SPACE TAXI

ALIENS ON EARTH

By Wendy Mass and Michael Brawer

Illustrated by Keith Frawley

LB

LITTLE, BROWN AND COMPANY
New York   Boston

Copyright © 2017 by Wendy Mass and Michael Brawer
Illustrations by Keith Frawley, based on the art of Elise Gravel

Cover art by Keith Frawley. Cover design by Kristina Iulo.
Cover copyright © 2017 by Hachette Book Group, Inc.

Little, Brown and Company
Hachette Book Group
1290 Avenue of the Americas, New York, NY 10104
Visit us at lb-kids.com

First Edition: May 2017

Little, Brown and Company is a division of Hachette Book Group, Inc. The Little, Brown name and logo are trademarks of Hachette Book Group, Inc.

The publisher is not responsible for websites (or their content) that are not owned by the publisher.

Library of Congress Cataloging-in-Publication Data
Names: Mass, Wendy, 1967– author. | Brawer, Michael, author. | Frawley, Keith, illustrator.
Title: Aliens on Earth / by Wendy Mass and Michael Brawer ;
illustrated by Keith Frawley, based on the art of Elise Gravel.
Description: First edition. | New York ; Boston : Little, Brown and Company, 2017. |
Series: Space taxi ; 6 | Summary: "When the space taxi navigation systems go down,
stranding dozens of aliens on Earth, eight-year-old Intergalactic Security Force
deputy Archie needs to think quickly to keep them hidden from his unsuspecting
neighbors!" —Provided by publisher.
Identifiers: LCCN 2016031989| ISBN 9780316308427 (hardback) |
ISBN 9780316308465 (trade pbk.) | ISBN 9780316308434 (ebk.)
Subjects: | CYAC: Interplanetary voyages—Fiction. | Adventure and adventurers—Fiction. |
Fathers and sons—Fiction. | Science fiction. | BISAC: JUVENILE FICTION / Science Fiction. |
JUVENILE FICTION / Science & Technology. | JUVENILE FICTION / Action & Adventure / General. |
JUVENILE FICTION / Animals / Cats.
Classification: LCC PZ7.M42355 Ali 2017 | DDC [Fic]—dc23
LC record available at https://lccn.loc.gov/2016031989

ISBNs: 978-0-316-30842-7 (hardcover), 978-0-316-30846-5 (pbk.), 978-0-316-30843-4 (ebook)

Printed in the United States of America

LSC-C

Hardcover: 10 9 8 7 6 5 4 3 2 1
Paperback: 10 9 8 7 6 5 4 3 2 1

To all the Space Taxi readers/passengers
who've come along for the ride,
this one's for you!
—WM and MB

For Shay and Josh.
—KF

CONTENTS

CHAPTER ONE:
The Furry Alien

One of my favorite parts of being Dad's space taxi copilot is the moment a new alien climbs into the backseat. Sometimes they jump, hop, slither, or roll in, too! That's the thing about aliens—you never know who you're going to get!

Usually the customer meets us at Barney's Bagels and Schmear, but today we're picking up an alien with the strangest name of any I've met so far. I couldn't believe it when Minerva sent Dad the assignment. His name is—wait for it—*Toe Fungus.*

Toe. Fungus.

I am *not* kidding. That is his real name. We're taking him back to his home, a small planet in the Sombrero Galaxy.

A thrill buzzes through me when Dad parks at the pickup location, a large warehouse by the river. This is the first time I've been to this part of town. The riverfront is full of old couches with torn cushions, a broken-down bumper car from an amusement park, and rubber tires laid out in a pattern perfect for jumping from one to the next. Dad has to pull me away from those. Mom says the riverfront is "no place for a child," but I think it's *exactly* the place for a child. This place rocks!

We knock on the dented metal door of the warehouse. While we're waiting, I say, "I bet this Toe Fungus guy is really hairy and smells like freshly baked chocolate chip cookies." I pause, then add, "And I bet he sings instead of talks."

Dad chuckles. "No way. He's probably two feet tall, with scales instead of skin. And really wonky toes, of course."

"Of course," I reply.

"But he doesn't sing," Dad says, knocking again. "He can only make clicking sounds with his tongue."

I grin. This is a fun game. We can call it *Guess That Alien!* Although I'm pretty sure my guess will be right.

The door opens an inch. A black-gloved hand shoots out, palm open.

Dad pulls out his space taxi driver ID card and hands it over. He is used to this. Aliens can't just go with anyone who rings their bell. What if that person was just selling Girl Scout cookies or stopping to ask directions and then an alien suddenly opened the door? 99.99 percent of people on Earth don't know there is life on other planets; Dad says that one day humans will be ready for it, but not yet. That's why alien visitors usually have their business meetings in out-of-the-way places like this.

The arm disappears from view, and a few seconds later the door swings open. It is very dark inside the warehouse, so we hear the alien before we see him. And he's singing a rap song!

"Welcome, driver of the sky, how nice of you to come on by!"

The alien steps out of the doorway and into the sunlight, a briefcase in his no-longer-gloved hand. The distinct odor of chocolate wafts out with him.

Dad turns toward me, his hands on his hips. "Archie Morningstar, you cheated!"

I laugh. "Maybe it was a lucky guess!" But truthfully, Pockets looked up his species for me before Dad and I left the apartment this morning, which is why I knew so much about him. Pockets was going to come with us, but he had some last-minute police business to take care of and closed himself in his office (otherwise known as my closet!) instead. When you're a highly decorated officer with the Intergalactic Security Force, your work always comes before a routine taxi run.

Besides singing and smelling like cookies, the alien is in fact covered completely in thick, brown, fur-like hair. Dad was right about the toes, though. Big and green—definitely wonky. And his height—he only comes up to my hip. Basically, he looks like a big stuffed animal.

After one last race through the obstacle course of tires (which Toe Fungus does with me!) we drive down to the airfield. We are eighth in line for takeoff.

"Why is the airfield so crowded today?" I ask, unrolling the space map that helps me navigate our trips.

Dad finishes his pre-flight checklist and says, "Actually, we have Pockets to thank for that. Now that everyone can use Camo-It-Now to disguise their Space Taxis, more drivers have been stopping here to refuel."

Minerva buzzes onto the line. "Good morning, Morningstars!" she says cheerily.

From the backseat, Toe Fungus sings out, "Good morning to you! The sky is so blue!"

Minerva gives a hesitant squeak like she's not sure what to make of our singing passenger. "Um, it certainly is?" she says. "Busy day today, so—" Her voice cuts off.

"Minerva?" Dad asks.

After a few seconds of silence, she comes back on. "Stand by for a public announcement."

Dad throws me a worried glance and flips the com line to PUBLIC.

Toe Fungus begins to hum. The tune is catchy and I find myself humming along. But Dad's increasingly worried expression stops me. "Is everything okay?" No one has moved forward in the line. "Why isn't anyone taking off?"

The com line crackles and Dad says, "I think we're about to find out."

CHAPTER TWO:
Trapped on Earth

"Attention all space taxi drivers and co-pilots." It's Minerva again, but she sounds very stern and her voice isn't nearly as squeaky as usual. "The entire fleet is grounded until further notice. A giant solar flare is heading toward Earth. It will reach us in six minutes, affecting all the satellites in Earth's orbit, and disrupting electronic devices of human and alien origin, including your taxi navigation systems and communication between the taxis and Home Base."

Dad and I look at each other in alarm.

Minerva continues. "Buses will arrive in two minutes to take all the passengers to Barney's. Barney is currently clearing out all the human customers. You will wait there for further instructions."

Toe Fungus finally stops humming.

"Please remain calm," Minerva says. "Once the solar storm passes, we'll get everyone back into space."

"I'm sure it will pass in a few hours," Dad assures Toe. "We'll get you on your way home very soon."

"What's a solar flare?" I ask Dad. "Does that mean the sun is in trouble?"

He shakes his head. "Picture the hot gases from the sun rising up like a tornado and shooting out into space."

My eyes widen.

"Don't worry, it's not as scary as it sounds. This one is just a little stronger than most."

One of the other taxi drivers buzzes in. It's Simon, an old buddy of Dad's. "How long do you expect us to be stuck on the ground?" he asks Minerva. "I've got an anti-ox in here. She was only supposed to be on Earth an hour."

Minerva doesn't answer right away.

"What's an anti-ox?" I whisper to Dad.

"It's what we call any species who can't breathe the oxygen in our air. They're allergic to it, so they don't usually come to Earth. Must have been on a short layover."

Minerva finally answers. "The Intergalactic Weather Station estimates at least a day or two for our equipment to recover. Until then, all the extra solar energy will make our readings inaccurate. You could aim for the Delta Quadrant and wind up in the Horsehead Nebula."

At that news I could hear groans coming from each com line. I glance behind me to see a long yellow bus pull into the airfield. It pulls up next to the line of taxis.

"Once again, stay calm and await further news at Barney's. Do not let your passengers be seen by earthlings."

A lot more grumbling follows, but one by one the drivers start moving their taxis off the runway. I hear a few complain about losing their place in line.

"I need to send word to Pockets," Dad says, parking and pulling out his phone. "He needs to know that he'll be cut off from Friskopolus and the rest of the ISF."

But before he can dial, the phone rings and Pockets' voice fills the car. "Good, I caught you. Solar storm headed this way. A big one. Meet me at Barney's." He hangs up, then calls right back. "Order me a tuna sandwich if you get there first." Then he hangs up again.

"Well," Dad says, slipping his soon-to-be-useless phone into his pocket, "guess I don't need to call him after all."

I watch out the window as aliens and their drivers stream from the taxis and climb onto the bus with an assortment of suitcases and bags. Many just have briefcases or handbags. They must have only been planning a day trip on Earth. I grab my space map and the lunch Mom packed us and we join the crowd. "This will be fun," Toe sings as we escort him to the bus. "Our adventure's just begun!"

The bus ride to Barney's is insane. Between my visits to Akbar's Floating Rest Stop and our ISF missions, I've seen a lot of different aliens. But never this many different kinds in this small a space. It's not working out so well.

"Get your giant foot off my ear!" a slug-bot in the third row warns a uni-pod. "Or I'll slime you so bad you'll be pulling goop out of your ear for a year."

The uni-pod tries to hop down the aisle away from the slugbot, but he gets wedged between two morphdoodles whose heads grow and shrink each time the bus hits a pothole.

It's also very loud, as everyone wants to use these last few seconds to tell whoever is waiting for them that they'll be late. I try not to stare at one alien who's having a very heated discussion with his thumb. There must be some kind of communication device hidden in there, but I can't see it from where I'm sitting, squished between Dad and Toe and Toe's suitcase.

Two rows in front of me I can see the top of what looks like a plastic blue bubble. When I peek over I'm surprised to see that inside that bubble is a girl sitting cross-legged, reading a book!

Now *that's* a new one for me! Other than the bubble—and if you overlook the pointy ears and two extra fingers—she looks like she could be a regular human girl.

"Do you need to call anyone, Toe?" Dad asks while also giving me a look that clearly says, *It's not polite to stare.* I sit back down in my seat.

Toe shakes his head. His fur gets in my mouth and I have to spit out a clump. (This is not as gross as it sounds. I'm used to it, since Pockets still sheds a lot.)

Then, suddenly, the bus goes quiet. Time's up and all the devices have cut out! I thought I'd feel something when the solar flare hit, like a wave of heat or a burst of light, but I don't feel anything. Some of the aliens shudder, and one of them burps and doesn't say "excuse me."

Then the eating begins. Maybe without the electronics to keep them busy, they realized they were hungry. Or maybe they're just eating to pass the time. Some of the food smells sweet and fruity, but the stuff that smells like raw fish (and probably *is* raw fish) overwhelms the rest and I try not to gag. It's *almost* worse than the slog-eating contest we went to on Akbar's.

We finally get to Barney's, and everyone climbs over each other to get out. The taxi drivers try to keep order, but it's impossible. The three of us wait until everyone else pushes by before we even try to stand up.

The bus is a mess. Half-eaten globs of goop drip from the seats, and something that looks like thick spaghetti dangles from the ceiling. The cushion on the seat

across from us is all sliced up, compliments of the porcupine-like alien who was unable to keep his spiky legs still enough.

The bus driver—a burly man with a mustache—stands and turns around. Since he works for the space taxi company, he clearly knows aliens exist. But his eyes widen and his face begins to turn purple as he takes in the condition of his bus. Dad, Toe, and I hurry past him, not wanting to be anywhere nearby when he sees the puddle on the floor of the back row. I don't even want to KNOW what *that* is!

The chaos continues inside the restaurant. It takes a lot to get Barney worked up, but right now he's shouting at the slugbot to stop leaving a trail of slime over the sandwiches he's laid out on the front counter.

Aliens and luggage are strewn across the room. A few aliens have spread out blankets and, unbelievably, are trying to nap! Two thin, pink alien women are fighting over the last pack of ketchup for their French fries.

I spot the bubble alien sitting alone in a corner, hugging her knees and looking around with wide eyes. She's younger than I thought, probably around my age. It's hard to tell with aliens, though. They may be a hundred years old but just grow slowly. This girl could be old enough to be my great-great-great-grandmother!

I'm about to go over and tell her she doesn't have to be scared, but then Simon, Dad's taxi driver friend, moves to stand in front of her and protect her from all the activity. Seeing Simon makes me realize that the girl is the anti-ox! The bubble must be keeping the air away from her.

We don't see Pockets anywhere, so Dad goes up to the counter to order a sandwich for him before the restaurant runs out of tuna and Pockets loses his mind.

"So…" I say to Toe, who is doing his best to stay out of the way of the other aliens, too. "What brought you to Earth?" I have to nearly shout to be heard.

"Back on Crollis 9 I'm studying to teach," he sings. "Math and science and mostly speech. Got a one-month gig at a school on Earth where I thought they'd find me weird or scary, but they thought I was just a kid who's really hairy!"

I peer at him up close. It's hard to believe

any kid would think he was human, but judging from how Penny treats Pockets, little kids see what they want to see. What *I* see is a cool, furry, singing alien who makes me smile.

Dad joins us, tuna sandwich in hand. "Pockets show up yet?"

As though he's heard his name (which he may have—he has excellent hearing), Pockets bursts through the door. His fur is wild and windblown, and I'm sure he raced all the way here. He stares at the scene around him and puts his paw in his mouth. A sharp whistle pierces the air. Everyone stops their eating/playing/sleeping/arguing and turns to look.

Holding his badge high over his head, Pockets announces, "As the only agent of the ISF currently on Earth, I am in charge of this sensitive situation."

But the aliens aren't ready to let Pockets talk. "I really need to get back to Yargon Prime," the uni-pod calls out. "I have an important business meeting tomorrow."

"Yeah, yeah," a lizard-like alien says with a dismissive wave. He has a few more legs than I think a lizard is normally allotted. "*I've* got my kid's birthday party. He's turning six hundred and twenty-one, and if I miss it, I'll never forgive myself. You can't get those early days back."

Others begin shouting out all the reasons they have to leave Earth, and Pockets whistles again and holds up his paw. "I understand having to wait is hard for everyone. But it's better than being stuck in space and having the taxi you were riding in suddenly stall out and drift aimlessly until it bangs into an asteroid. Right?"

The aliens grunt and shuffle their feet, which I take as a sign of their agreement.

Pockets continues. "Judging from the scene before me, we clearly cannot keep all of you together in one place. Each driver will be taking home whatever alien was in his or her taxi at the time of the solar flare. Home Base will alert you when the airfield has reopened."

At the news of unexpected houseguests, it's the drivers' turn to complain. Even Dad starts to protest. After all, we've got Penny to consider. She can't know about aliens until she's old enough to keep secrets better.

Pockets holds up his paw again. "Every driver will be paid double his or her salary to help cover the cost of feeding and housing your guests."

That quiets them down.

"Because of the damage to the bus, however, the bus company refuses to bring you to your temporary homes around the city. Normally it would be up to the ISF to decide how to get you there without attracting attention, but I have lost my connection with the chief."

"Also known as his *father*," I whisper to Toe.

Pockets motions with his paw for Dad to toss him the sandwich, so he does. "I'm open to suggestions," he tells the room. "It's not like we can just march you all down the center of Main Street in bright sunlight!"

"We can just wait till dark to sneak 'em out," one of the drivers suggests.

Pockets shakes his head. "Can't wait that long. Barney's is meant to be a short-term waiting area, and we are well over our maximum occupancy. The food supply is dwindling, and we're way too exposed in the middle of the city like this."

"Can you use the Atomic Assembler on them?" I ask. "You could make all the aliens look like humans." After being turned into an alien on Tri-Dark last month, I still sometimes feel like my arms are extra long!

Pockets bites into his sandwich and shakes his head. "None of my high-tech gadgets will work."

"Oh, right. I forgot." I think about the problem for a minute, and about what Toe told me about blending in. Then it hits me...maybe there's a way aliens CAN march down the middle of Main Street in bright sunlight after all!

CHaPTER THREE:
Aliens on Parade

"*A parade?*" Pockets asks. He reaches for his sandwich and then frowns when he sees only crumbs are left. "How could we hold a parade? Everyone would see us."

I shake my head. "Not a regular parade, a *costume* parade. Or, at least that's what people will *think* they're seeing. We can put up posters around the area advertising a costume parade and a prize for the craziest outfit. If regular people join in, that will be even better."

"I think it can work!" Dad says. "The drivers would march alongside their aliens, and then each group can veer off when they reach their homes."

"Let's do it!" Pockets declares.

Then things happen fast!

First, Pockets announces the plan to the room, giving me credit for coming up with it, which makes me feel very grown-up. Since all the cell phone signals are knocked out, the drivers line up to use Barney's land-line phone to ask their relatives to bring them old Halloween costumes. Toe whips out some crayons and he and some of the more artistic aliens make posters on the back of Barney's paper menus. Barney's staff hurries outside to tape them up on telephone poles along the parade route.

I'm a bit jealous they get to go outside on such a nice Saturday afternoon. I may not have mentioned the smell in the hot, overpacked restaurant, but *ohh*, the smell. It's a cross between festering garbage and wet earwax. It's totally not the aliens' faults that their bodies react with our atmosphere this way. Even Toe's natural chocolate chip cookie odor can't make a dent in the stench.

I want to wear my baseball uniform as my costume, but since Mom is out at the park with Penny, we can't reach her.

Pockets suggests Dad and I look in Barney's back room to see what we can put together, but the aliens have eaten or taken everything in sight, even the coffee beans and sugar packets. They left exactly one paper hat and one bag of flour (which we found toppled over and hidden behind a cabinet). This explains why Dad is now dressed as a chef and I'm a ghost—a ghost who's going to be picking flour out of his hair and ears for weeks!

Within an hour, we're lining up outside Barney's to march down the middle of the street. Pockets organizes everyone so that the people who live closest are in the front of the parade and can just leave the line when their houses come up. That way it's nice and orderly. I would never have thought of that, but that's why he's the boss!

Small groups and families begin joining us, dressed as firefighters and witches and baseball players and ducks. It's awesome! Even more people line up on the sidewalks to watch, never guessing that they're looking right at aliens from planets across the entire universe. I feel bad that we couldn't reach Mom. Penny would have loved this.

Barney himself leads the parade. Someone gave him a pink wig to cover his bald head. The bagpipe he's playing must be his, though; I don't think many people have one lying around! Someone brought candy and is now throwing it out to the crowd as the parade passes by.

We've gotten about a block down the street when I hear a voice shout, "Archie!"

I scan the crowd to see where it came from. "Mom!"

She waves from the sidewalk. She must have seen one of the signs. When Penny sees me and Dad, she pulls free of Mom's hand and runs to join us.

Her eyes are wide with wonder as she takes in all the different aliens, who she no doubt believes are people in costume. "Why are you all white, Archie?" she asks when she reaches us. I'm still getting used to her speaking in full sentences!

"I'm a ghost." I hold up my hands and wiggle my fingers. "Boo!"

She pretends to jump in fright. Then she notices Pockets marching a few rows ahead of us and loses interest in me. "Pockets!" she shouts, and runs over to him.

"Don't take it personally," Dad says with a grin. "I didn't even get a hello!"

"She sure loves that cat," I say.

"She does indeed."

"How are we going to explain Toe coming to stay with us?" I look around for him and see him a few yards behind us, chatting with one of the pink ladies.

"I was thinking about that," Dad says as we turn the corner from Main to Elm. "If Toe doesn't speak, maybe we can pass him off as a large, fluffy stuffed animal?"

I glance back again. I can hear Toe singing from here. "Pretty sure we can't keep him quiet for very long."

"Yeah, probably not."

"He said the kids he taught at school thought he was just a hairy person. Maybe that's what Penny will think."

"As long as she doesn't see his feet!"

Small groups are now starting to slip away from the parade and into apartment buildings along the route. I see Simon and Bubble Girl (as I've started to call her) break off next. He's dressed as a farmer, in a straw hat and overalls. I watch in awe as she rolls down the street next to him, like a hamster in a wheel, except she's not walking on all fours. She has a small duffel bag attached to the side of the bubble with magnets. I don't see an opening in the bubble, but there must be one or else she wouldn't be able to get anything out of her bag.

They turn the corner onto a side street and disappear into one of the houses. No one even turns to watch. They must think it's just two regular people in costume. The plan is working!

We live pretty far from Barney's, so most of the others are gone by the time our turn comes. Mom has joined Pockets and Penny. As soon as we are in front of our building, she scoops up Penny and we all step to the sidewalk so the rest of the group can continue.

Our neighbor Mr. Goldblatt is on the stoop watching the parade with his little dog, Luna. Even though she can't see very well because she's so old, Luna immediately sniffs at Pockets, who hisses in response and scrambles backward. I'd have thought that going to Canis—the dog planet—would have cured Pockets of his fear of dogs, but nope.

Luna's head whirls around as she picks up an unfamiliar scent. But before she can get too close to our new houseguest, Dad ushers Toe into the building and up the stairs to our apartment.

"Penny," Dad says once we're all inside, "this is our new friend, Toe. He's going to be staying with us for a day or two."

Mom leans toward Dad and whispers, "We haven't had a houseguest since Bubba from Belora Prime lived under the sink. Whatever happened to that little guy?"

"He's still there," Dad whispers back.

Mom's eyes widen.

"Kidding," Dad says, grinning. "He's not. At least I don't *think* he is."

Penny steps a little closer to Mom and looks shyly over at Toe. She makes friends very easily. It's a gift she has. I start counting backward from ten in my head. *Ten... nine...* She tilts her head toward him and sniffs. "Chocolate chip cookie?" *Eight... seven...* She moves closer to him, sniffing him some more. I notice they're about the same height. Toe smiles and sings, "Penny is a lovely name. Would you like to play a game?"

Mom looks amused by how Toe sings, but Penny squeals with delight, grabs Toe's hand, and runs into the living room, where the board games are piled up. I knew I wouldn't even make it down to one before she found herself a new best friend. The next time we see him, Toe's fur is braided, his nails are painted purple (guess she wasn't freaked out by the wonky toes!), and he's wearing a skirt made out of newspaper.

Pockets takes one look at him, mutters, "Better him than me," and races from the room.

CHaPteR FouR:
Gone Missing

Toe sleeps standing up. He must have a very good sense of balance. Earlier this morning Penny and I tried standing up and closing our eyes, but we kept falling into each other and crashing to the floor. Mom made us stop before we smashed our heads together or woke Toe or Mr. Goldblatt below us.

Toe is still sleeping right now, in the middle of my room, even though the sun is streaming through the window and Dad is playing his music in the kitchen. Penny is sitting at Toe's feet, waiting impatiently for him to wake up and play with her. I think she tired him out yesterday. By the time night fell, his songs had started to get shorter, like, "Off to bed, or fall on head" and "Long day, must dream away."

Pockets has been acting strange. I have a feeling that not being able to talk to his dad or the ISF is starting to really bother him. Since yesterday afternoon, he's only left my closet to eat, to check on Toe once or twice, and to see if there's any news on when systems will be up and running again. All night I heard his paws clacking on the keyboard, but I never saw what he was working on.

Suddenly Penny shouts, "Toe's waking up!" I happily put down my math homework (I like math and all, but I like aliens in my bedroom better!) and hurry over. Toe's toes do this weird stretchy thing, then snap back into place. His shoulders lift up, then settle down again. Then his eyes fly open and he smiles.

"Good morning to you! The sky is so blue and we have so much to do!"

Penny claps her hands together and she and Toe run off to build a castle out of empty toilet paper rolls. I'm about to go back to tackling the next problem ($8 + 4 = 3 \times$ __?)

when Dad comes rushing in. He's holding the house phone. "Where's Pockets?"

I point to the closet. Dad pulls open the door.

"Hey," Pockets says with a scowl. "Heard of knocking? Common courtesy!"

Papers are strewn all over the floor around him, but other than that, his office is unusually clean. Most of his gadgets and gizmos are piled in a cardboard box on the floor. Maybe he figures he doesn't need so much stuff around since the solar flare prevents it from working. I want to ask Pockets if he's okay or if he wants to talk about anything, but Dad obviously needs him right now.

"I'll knock next time," Dad promises, "but this can't wait." He hands Pockets the phone.

A few seconds later I hear Pockets shout, "Wait, what? Who's where? When?"

That's a lot of *W* questions!

A minute later Pockets hangs up, tosses the phone onto the bed, and says, "Get dressed fast. We have a missing alien."

Fifteen minutes later, Dad, Pockets, and I are standing on Simon's front porch. The missing alien is Bubble Girl! Toe asked to come, but Pockets didn't want to risk anyone seeing him. Just because a four-year-old believes he's human doesn't mean adults will.

Simon explains what happened. "Me and the wife were having our usual breakfast of eggs and salami. We kept calling upstairs for the little gal to roll on down for something to eat. We knew she didn't sleep too well, because all night long we could hear her rolling around up there. Felt sorry for the kid, stuck in that bubble thing, but what could we do? The air is the air, ya know?"

"Go on," Pockets says impatiently.

"So we went up to check on her and found the window open. She must have pushed herself out and rolled down the roof and taken off. Took her small bag with her."

"Why do you think she left?" Pockets asks.

"No idea," Simon says. "But if she cracked her bubble on the way down, the air inside from her home planet would start to leak out, and the oxygen would get in."

My stomach flip-flops like it does when

the taxi goes through a wormhole. "What happens when an anti-ox comes into contact with oxygen?" I ask.

"It's different for each species," Simon replies. "Sometimes the effects can be mild, like an itchy rash. But sometimes, well, let's just say they don't recover."

Pockets growls. Dad and I exchange a look. We've heard that growl before. It's never a good sign. Pockets begins to pace in circles. "I could use six different devices to find her if this solar storm hadn't happened."

I'm about to point out that she wouldn't still *be* on Earth if the solar storm hadn't happened, but I figure that wouldn't be too helpful.

Pockets continues to pace. "I can't even

track her the old-fashioned way because I never got a whiff of her yesterday. If she approaches a human for help, or someone spots her, the results will be disastrous."

I clear my throat. "Um, Pockets? Why would it be so bad if people on Earth knew about aliens? I mean, *we* all know, and it's not like we freaked out or anything."

Dad puts his hand on my shoulder. "Son, it's more complicated than that. Humans *will* find out that they're not alone in the universe one day, but not until we understand how to work together in harmony with the aliens. Certainly there are people who can handle the truth, but those aren't the ones we're worried about."

I nod. I think I understand.

"Focus, people," Pockets says, waving his

paws. "Runaways usually go somewhere they're familiar with. We need to follow the parade route back to Barney's. Simon, you stay here in case she returns."

He digs out four walkie-talkies from one of his many chest pockets and hands one to Simon. "Alert me if you hear anything. A little solar storm won't keep *us* quiet!" He tosses them to the rest of us and we set out.

Confetti and glitter and stray candy still line the parade route, so it's easy to retrace our steps. As we follow the trail backward, I start to notice tiny movements—a curtain shifting here, a branch rustling there, the flash of a yellow eye in a garage window, the smell of something sour that makes me crinkle my nose.

At first Pockets' super senses keep making him stop and pivot every few feet, too, his tail low and ears back. It always turns out to be just a bored or lonely alien, though, and never the one we're looking for. With no sign of Bubble Girl, I admit I'm getting a little worried. Even if she didn't spring a leak, what if she rolled right into a lake or something? Can the bubble float?

"Don't look so worried," Dad says, putting his hand on my shoulder. "She's in good hands with Pockets on the case. That cat ALWAYS gets his man. Or in this case, his girl in a bubble."

Chapter Five:
A Clue!

After checking behind dumpsters and telephone poles and storage sheds, we wind up back at Barney's. I'm surprised to see that everything looks totally normal. The tables and chairs have all been set back up, and regular people are having nice breakfasts of bagels and steaming plates of eggs. Since no taxis can land, there aren't any new aliens trying to blend in while they await pickup.

Pockets heads directly for the self-serve shelf and grabs a plate of tuna. Then he seems to remember that he's supposed to be a regular cat and gets down on all four paws to lick it off the plate.

"Hiya, Mr. Morningstar," the young woman at the counter says. I've never seen her here before. She has long, straight yellow hair and earrings up and down both ears.

"Good morning, Vanya," Dad replies with a smile. "I haven't seen you in a few months. Is Barney here?"

"Nope. Dad is exhausted from all the

excitement yesterday, so I'm helping out."
She glances around to make sure no one
can hear. "I heard it got pretty wild."

Dad leans in. "That it did. Hey, did you
see an alien girl about my son's age in here
earlier? She would have been inside a blue
bubble."

"So, you know, hard to miss," I add.

She shakes her head and comes around
the side of the counter. "The only alien I've
seen this morning was a tall, white-haired
man in a fancy gray suit. Didn't even know
he was an alien until he ordered some
pastries and a coffee and then started to
drink the coffee through his nose."

"Okay, that's really weird," I say.

"Yeah," she agrees. "I tried to make
small talk with him, you know, ask him

where he was staying during the storm, but before he could answer I turned away for, like, a second, and he was gone. Just slipped away without waiting for his change."

Dad looks quizzical. "I don't recall seeing a man like that yesterday. Do you, Archie?"

I think for a minute, then shake my head. "It was really crowded, though."

Even though Pockets is still acting like a regular cat, I can tell from the angle of his ears that he heard the conversation. He pretends to rub against my leg as he whispers to Vanya, "Let us know if he shows up again, or if the girl in the bubble does." He motions for me to give Vanya my walkie-talkie. I pull it off my belt loop and she slides it into her apron pocket.

"Will do," she says. Then she bends down and pets Pockets on the head. Smiling up at me, she says, "Your cat is so cute, how can you stand it?"

Pockets growls.

"You know he's not really my pet, right?" I ask.

She grins. "I know. But it's fun to make him squirm."

"It *is* fun to make him squirm!" I agree. I like this girl!

Vanya hands me and Dad free bagels (mine has chocolate chips in it, which makes me like her even more!) and Pockets nudges us firmly toward the door.

Once outside, we duck into the alley beside the store and Pockets drops the "I'm just a cute, innocent house pet" act and gets back to business. "Whoever that man is, he's not supposed to be wandering around." He pulls out his tablet and taps it angrily a few times, then tucks it away again. "I'd already know his identity by now if this was working!" He sighs. "We'll just have to keep doing this the old-fashioned way."

He holds up his walkie-talkie and presses the button. "Simon? You there? Any word?"

Only static comes through. Pockets tries again, with the same result.

"Do you think something could have happened to him?" Dad asks. "Maybe this goes deeper than an alien running away. Maybe she was taken! And now they've come back for Simon!"

Pockets shakes his head. "You've been watching too much television."

"Probably," Dad admits.

"Still, let's get back there," Pockets says. "Maybe the girl's shown up and we can get back to...well, to all the stuff we have to do."

He looks away as he says that. I get an unpleasant chill down my back but force myself not to jump to any conclusions. As my mom told me once when I used to worry a lot, "Nothing's wrong till something's wrong." Right now we already have one real mystery on our hands, plus we need to get back to Toe. Who knows what Penny's done to him by now? I pick up the pace.

A few minutes later, Pockets pounds on Simon's door. It swings open. "Any luck?" Simon asks.

Pockets holds up the walkie-talkie. "Why didn't you answer?"

Simon reaches over to the hall table and grabs his walkie-talkie from under a pile of outgoing mail. "Oh, this thing? I didn't know what it was."

"Really?" I can't help saying. "I got my first walkie-talkie when I was five."

Dad leans toward me. "Simon spent most of his childhood away from Earth. His father ran the taxi operations at Home Base."

Well, that explains it.

"Sorry I missed your call," Simon says. "But I told your ISF buddy that I didn't have any more news. Figured he'd pass that on."

Pockets' ears flatten. "I didn't send anyone."

"No?" Simon looks surprised.

"White-haired guy in a fancy gray suit?" Pockets asks.

"Yup. You ISF agents must make a good living to afford high-quality threads like that."

Pockets ignores that comment and asks, "Did he drink with his nose?"

"What? No—I mean, I don't know. He wasn't drinking anything."

"What exactly did he say?" Pockets presses.

"He just asked to see the girl, and when I said she wasn't here anymore, he thanked me politely and left."

"That's it?" Pockets asks. He sits down on the porch and begins jotting down notes on a notepad. His pencil tip breaks, and that sends him nearly over the edge. He is not handling this low-tech lifestyle very well. He angrily pulls out another pencil and continues scribbling away. After a full minute of Pockets ignoring the rest of us, Dad and Simon strike up a conversation about boring space taxi stuff like wind drag and the importance of always having a roll of duct tape to patch torn hoses. I'm curious to see the girl's escape route. I back off the porch.

"Be right back," I tell Dad, and then hurry over to the side of the house, where Simon pointed earlier.

I tilt my head back and can see the still-open window. It must have been a tight squeeze. And the roof is pretty steep. At some point she would have had to soar through the air in order to reach the ground. I hope that bubble can bounce!

About halfway up the house I spot something yellow—fabric? paper?—stuck behind the rusty brown drainpipe that runs down from the gutter to the ground. At this distance I can't tell what it is. Part of Bubble Girl's duffel that ripped off on her way down? I try to remember what color that was, but can't. It could be nothing, or it could be a clue.

"Pockets?" I call out. "Can you climb a drainpipe?"

CHaPTeR SiX:
Cracking the Code

Yup, Pockets can climb a drainpipe. But he doesn't even need to. He just crouches low and then leaps up into the air, grabbing the yellow object with his teeth. For such a huge cat, he lands with only the slightest *plop*.

Dad pulls the object out of Pockets' mouth. It does turn out to be paper—a flyer or an ad for something. Only it's written in some foreign language. Pockets smooths it out on the ground, turns it a quarter turn, studies it, then turns it again. I'm preparing for that growl of frustration that's become so common since yesterday, but instead he just sighs and hangs his head.

"It's my own fault," he says. "This could be the clue we need, but I didn't pay enough attention in my classes at the ISF Academy. I figured, why should I bother to learn all those languages when all I have to do is plug them into my tablet or stick in my Translate-Ear? Now I know why."

I awkwardly pat him on the shoulder. "Don't feel too bad. A solar storm knocking out all your equipment almost never happens, right? And hey, Toe told me he's studying to be a teacher. I bet he knows something about alien languages."

We get home to find everyone around the kitchen table. Mom deposits a fresh stack of pancakes in front of Toe, who is clutching his belly. "I couldn't eat one more bite," he sings when he sees us. "Pancakes this good are a total delight!"

"Mom's pancakes are definitely the best," I agree. I give Toe a quick once-over to make sure Penny hasn't decided to pierce his ears or strap her purple dragon to his back. Except for the fact that his wavy fur has been brushed straight, he looks pretty much how we left him.

Now back to being unable to speak since Penny is around, Pockets heads into the living room and curls up in a sunny spot. Ten seconds later, he's snoring. Whatever else is bothering him, it can't compete with his need to sleep.

Toe gets to work on the flyer while Dad and I help ourselves to his breakfast. Barney's bagels are good, but nothing compares to Mom's pancakes. Bored, Penny wanders off into the living room and curls up next to Pockets. His snores are now mixed with purrs. Penny can always get him to purr, even in his sleep!

"Archie," Toe sings after making sure Penny can't hear the question, "does Pockets have a copy of *Aliens 'R' Us*?"

"He has a lot of books," I reply. "I'll go

look." I stop halfway out of the room. "I just rhymed! Well, sort of!"

Toe grins. "You're a poet and don't know it!"

Between missions, Pockets likes for us to take him to the local public library. He always comes home with an armload of books on all different topics. But now all his books are packed in one big box, and a suitcase sits in the middle of the closet floor. With all his built-in pockets to carry stuff, Pockets *never* needs a suitcase. Unless... unless he's going away on a long trip and hasn't told us? Is that what's bothering him?

I sort through the books until I find the one Toe asked about. It must be one Pockets brought from home. A book describing all these different aliens would be handy to have on our visits to Akbar's. Actually, it would have been handy to have yesterday at *Barney's*!

I bring it back to the kitchen and Toe flips to a section at the end. It has a chart with all the letters of the alphabet in different boxes. He points to the page and sings, "Sorry to take so long. We were doing this all wrong! It's not a language, it's a code! That is what the book here showed. Every letter stands for another. Is it okay if I hug your mother?"

He jumps up, hugs a surprised Mom, and sits back down. I'm pretty sure he did that just so his song would rhyme!

Dad picks up the flyer. "So if A equals Z, and B equals Y, and C equals X, etc., then this should be easy to figure out!"

He grabs pencils from the drawer and we all begin writing the real letters under the fake ones. Slowly a message emerges.

Come to 37 Main Street and make new friends! B.U.R.P. will be hiring for many new positions. Salary dependent on experience and how much we like you. Cookies and lemonade will be served.

"Someone is recruiting for B.U.R.P.!" Dad exclaims. "On Earth!" He shudders. "B.U.R.P. has never made it this far into the galaxy before. We thought we were safe."

"And the girl had this flyer," I remind him. "That's where she went—to the meeting!" As hard as it is to believe that the girl would want to work for the universe's most villainous villains, one thing I've learned from being an ISF deputy is that you can't judge people by how they look. And sometimes the bad guys aren't always all bad, like the first time we saw Sebastian and he was feeding hungry cats. It can be confusing who to trust.

Toe shouts, "We figured it out, without a doubt!"

From his spot on the living room floor, Pockets springs up into the air. "You figured it out?" he shouts before hitting the ground at a run. Toe is happy to show him the newly decoded flyer.

I'm the only one who notices Penny sitting in the center of the living room floor, her mouth hanging open.

CHAPTER SEVEN:
Secrets and Sisters

I'm only half listening as Dad calls the other taxi drivers to find out if any of their houseguests got the same flyer. Four aliens admit they got one but say they couldn't read it and threw it out. Another figured it out (he has a brain the size of a watermelon) but has never heard of B.U.R.P. because he is from a very peaceful planet where the worst crime is not saying hello when you pass someone on the street.

Meanwhile, Pockets and Toe have gone into my room to make a plan to sneak into the meeting. I'm not sure if Pockets is more worried about B.U.R.P. being on Earth, Bubble Girl's bubble leaking, or his upcoming secret trip. I'm worried about all those things, too, but mostly I'm worried about Penny.

I haven't taken my eyes off her. Her own eyes are all watery from holding them open so wide. My heart is pounding hard. All this time we've been keeping Pockets' secret so that Penny wouldn't blow his cover by telling everyone that her giant pet cat is actually a fairly regular-sized police cat from another planet.

What we *should* have been thinking about is how she would handle the news when she actually got it. After hearing him shout, she looks totally shocked. Should I tell her that she only *thought* she heard Pockets talk? That she'd fallen asleep and dreamt it? I need to do something.

I glance away from her and say, "Mom, Dad, um, we have a problem."

"If B.U.R.P. is really here," Dad says, "we have more than *one* problem."

Mom looks up from the sink. "What's wrong, Archie?"

I point down the hall to Penny, who chooses that moment to stand up. Her legs wobble under her. I'm afraid that she's going fall or burst into tears. But to my surprise, she races down the hall, throws open my bedroom door, and shouts, "I knew it! I knew one day you would talk!"

Mom, Dad, and I reach my room in time to see her wrap her arms around a stunned Pockets. "You can talk now! You can talk!"

"Um, meow?" Pockets manages to reply, as we watch helplessly from the doorway.

Mom moves first. She hurries in and kneels down to peel Penny off of Pockets, but Penny's not letting go. "Mommy, Daddy, Archie! Pockets has learned how to talk! Wait till I tell my friends at school!"

Dad sighs. "And there it is."

Mom looks over at us. "Let me handle this," she says, finally succeeding in prying Penny off of Pockets. "You all have to get moving if you want to make it to the meeting in time."

Pockets doesn't need to be told twice. He's out the front door before Mom even finishes her sentence. Dad gives Penny a pat on the head and says, "Love you, little girl." His eyes are watery. The last of his children will soon know the secret he's kept for all these years. It's a big day for him, too. I turn to follow Pockets, but Dad can't seem to move.

Toe puts one furry hand on Dad's arm. "I promise Penny will be okay. You knew it would happen someday. Your daughter is smart, with a big, trusting heart."

"Thank you," Dad says, and I can tell he means it. He strokes Penny's hair one more time, then we run to catch up to Pockets. The meeting location is downtown, very close to Barney's. We probably even passed by it already this morning!

Pockets comes to a sudden stop. "There!" he says, pointing. I follow his paw but only see a dirt lot between two buildings. Dad checks the address on the flyer, then looks at the numbers on the front of the two buildings.

"Huh," Dad says. "Whatever building used to be here isn't here anymore."

"We're not looking for a building," Pockets says.

"We're not?" I ask. I scan the area and see only one large tree, a few scraggly bushes, and a lot of dirt and yellow grass. "We must be too late, then. No one is here anymore."

Pockets shakes his head. "They're here, all right."

He marches to the large tree and then walks around to the back of it. We follow him. At first I don't see anything. He sticks out a paw and pushes on what looks to me like an ordinary lump in the tree trunk.

It's not an ordinary lump. A door swings

open, revealing a staircase. A staircase in a tree! I light up. I'm used to seeing unexpected and cool things on other planets, but this is in my own backyard, practically! I start to step inside but Pockets sticks out his paw again and blocks me.

"Wait," he commands. "I'll go first in case there are any nasty surprises waiting at the bottom."

I step aside, and we all follow Pockets down the dark, winding staircase. It smells clean and earthy, like you'd expect the inside of a tree to smell. As soon as Toe closes the door behind him, we are plunged into complete darkness. Pockets uses the laser on his tail to light our way.

After a minute of walking, we feel the stairs flatten out and we step off onto solid

ground again. A dim light reaches our eyes. What is waiting at the bottom is pretty much the complete *opposite* of a nasty surprise. Instead of stepping onto dirt like I expected, we are standing on soft grass and are surrounded by flowers and candles. Music wafts through the large open space and I smell freshly baked cinnamon rolls! The smell blends with Toe's natural odor and my stomach begins to growl.

Wide-eyed, Dad asks, "What *is* this place?"

A few seconds later, a man's voice calls out. "Welcome, visitor!" His words echo off the rock walls. "You must be here for the meeting."

CHapter Eight:
B.U.R.P. Underground

Pockets puts his paw to his lips and motions for us to step back onto the staircase, where we can blend into the dark. Then he steps forward alone, into the light. The man approaches from the other direction and we can now see him clearly. He is tall and wears a fancy gray suit. *Sigh.* I should have seen *that* coming.

"This is the B.U.R.P. recruitment meeting, right?" Pockets asks.

"It certainly is, Mr....?"

"You can just call me Pockets."

"Hello, Pockets," the man says. He is clutching red plastic cups in both hands. He holds one out to Pockets. "Would you like some lemonade? It's very refreshing."

"No, thank you," Pockets says. Then he grabs for the cup and gulps it down anyway. The man lifts his own cup and pours it straight into his nose! Dad and I shudder. Toe just tilts his head, fascinated.

"Well, Mr. Pockets, are you interested in a life of travel and excitement, full of surprises and riches?"

"Sure," Pockets says, tucking the empty cup into one of his pockets. "And you're the guy to get it for me?"

The man bows and says, "Agent Igor Zell. Been with B.U.R.P. for fifty years. As you can see around you, it's afforded me a wonderful lifestyle."

"You've lived underground on Earth for *fifty years*?" Pockets says, his eyes wide with surprise.

Agent Zell laughs. "Of course not. I only came to this backward little planet a few days ago on some business, and got stuck after the storm hit." He looks around him. "Stumbled into this place. Must have been an old storm cellar or something. Works great for my purposes. My partner just retired and I'm in the market for a new one. No one else has shown up, though."

"No one?" Pockets replies.

"Just you," Agent Zell confirms.

I pull on Dad's sleeve and whisper, "Does that mean Bubble Girl ran away after all?" I feel a little bad for referring to her out loud as Bubble Girl. I mean, I'm sure she has a name.

"I suppose it does," Dad agreed. "Which means she could be anywhere."

"Why don't you tell me about yourself?" Agent Zell asks Pockets as he eyes him up and down.

"One more question for you," Pockets says. "I heard your leader, Sebastian, has escaped capture. You wouldn't happen to know where he is, would you?"

I lean forward, awaiting Zell's reply. I'd like to see Sebastian again. Meeting someone who looks just like you is very strange.

But Zell only laughs. "The leader of B.U.R.P. is very secretive. I am certainly not privy to his whereabouts. Now, let's get down to business, shall we? Do you have any special skills that would help you thrive in the B.U.R.P. organization? Lock picking, perhaps? Or the ability to divide yourself in half and be in two places at once?"

Instead of answering, Pockets says, "Aren't you afraid that handing out flyers to strangers might be dangerous? How do you know you won't run into an ISF agent?"

Zell snorts. "All the way out here on Earth? They couldn't be bothered to make the trip."

Pockets whips out his badge and a pair of handcuffs. "That's what I thought about *you*. Guess we were both wrong."

Before Agent Zell can move, Pockets springs forward and lands behind him. He's about to snap on the handcuffs when Zell suddenly swells up to twice his size! Maybe he's the same species as the aliens on the bus whose heads kept changing size. His own head now grazes the ceiling!

Fortunately, Pockets is no stranger to last-minute surprises. He reaches into a pocket and pulls out what looks like a wad of chewed gum. Then he climbs right up Zell's body like it's a tree! Zell yelps and flails around to dislodge Pockets but only succeeds in knocking dirt off the ceiling and getting it in his eyes.

Pockets slaps the gum right on the back of Zell's neck. Within seconds, Zell is back to normal size, the handcuffs are on Zell's wrists, and Pockets is leading him to the stairs.

Zell glares when he finally notices the rest of us, then sneers at Pockets. "You're making a big mistake. No Earth jail will hold me." He wiggles his fingers. "I already erased my fingerprints, so you'll never pin any crimes on me. The neutralizer in that chewing gum will last only ten minutes, and you can't get me off the planet in that time."

"Maybe *I* can't," Pockets agrees. "But I know someone who can."

"He does?" I whisper to Dad as we climb back up after them. Well, Pockets is climbing. Zell is being pulled.

"I think he's bluffing," Dad whispers back. "Trying to psych him out."

"No, I'm not," Pockets says.

I always forget that super hearing of his!

"That's right, he's not," another voice echoes from above.

We step out into the bright sun. "Feemus!" I shout, throwing my arms around the president of Pockets' fan club. "What are you doing here?"

"How'd you land in the middle of a solar storm?" Dad asks.

The little red alien shrugs. "For Pockets I'll risk frying my electrical system."

"And?"

"Yeah, it's fried," Feemus says. He looks at Pockets adoringly. "But it was worth it. And I have a backup."

Pockets rolls his eyes and pushes Zell toward Feemus. "You know the drill."

Feemus nods. "I do indeed, oh fearless leader, oh wondrous example of amaze-i-tude."

"I don't think that word is real," Toe sings, "but I know just how you feel. The Morningstars, too, have been brave and true."

Feemus grunts and barely glances at us. I'm used to that from him. Never was there a more loyal president of anyone's fan club than Feemus. Pockets is a lucky cat. Even though he'll rarely give Feemus any credit. Having a fan club just embarrasses him too much.

Feemus freezes Agent Zell and tosses him into his little round spaceship, which he's hidden behind a bush. "His memory will be wiped," Feemus assures us. "Can't have a B.U.R.P. agent knowing where the greatest ISF agent who ever traveled the universe lives!"

Pockets opens his mouth to say something, but then closes it and gives a curt nod. That's as close to a thank-you as Feemus is likely to get. Pockets fishes the plastic cup out of his pocket, slips it into a plastic bag, and tosses it to Feemus. "Give this to the lab at ISF headquarters. They can analyze his prints and track down his previous crimes."

I shake my head in awe of Pockets' quick thinking in keeping that cup. If Agent Zell weren't frozen right now, I bet he'd be fuming.

Feemus salutes Pockets, and zips back into space.

We quickly continue checking the neighborhood for the girl. "Pockets, why can Feemus still freeze people and wipe their memories if no alien gadgets are supposed to work?"

"We all have inner gifts that nothing—not B.U.R.P. or a solar storm or time or distance from our loved ones—can take away," Pockets explains. "Like your dad's skill at flying space taxis, or yours at navigating, or how you help solve cases by seeing things that no one else sees."

I feel my cheeks redden under his praise. Pockets usually never says stuff like that. He definitely hasn't been himself these last few days. "Penny has gifts, too," I say. "Everyone likes her because she's so kind and friendly. I bet aliens other than you and Toe would like her, too, if she ever gets to meet them. But I know we're taking that slow."

"No need to take it slow," Toe sings, stepping between us. "The truth she does already know."

Dad stops when he hears that. "What do you mean?"

Toe points to a small playground across the street. Sitting on opposite ends of a see-saw are Penny and one large blue bubble with an alien girl inside.

CHAPTER NINE:
Hello and Good-bye

"How?" Pockets asks Mom when we reach them. *"When?"*

"Penny had a lot of questions about Pockets," Mom says, "so I tried to find you. You didn't answer the walkie-talkie."

"We were underground," Dad explains.

"It was very cool. I'll have to take you sometime now that it's free of B.U.R.P. agents."

Mom raises an eyebrow, likely wondering how being underground could be cool (although it *was* ten degrees cooler down there!). "Anyway, we stopped to swing for a few minutes, until Penny jumped off and said, 'Someone else is here.' I didn't see anyone, but sure enough, from up in the tree house came a kind of ripping sound. We went to check it out and found the missing alien. Unless there's another alien in a pink T-shirt inside a blue bubble."

"Nope, she's the only one," Pockets confirms.

"I asked the girl about the meeting

and she didn't know what I was talking about. She wasn't able to read that flyer."

Pockets' ears twitch. "Then why did she leave Simon's house?"

Mom smiles proudly at Penny. "I think she just needed a friend."

"What was the ripping sound you heard earlier?" Dad asks.

Pockets points to an empty roll of duct tape on the ground, and then up to the bubble. Now that we're so close, I can see a silver X shape on the inside of the bubble. She DID spring a leak! Duct tape really CAN fix anything!

Pockets runs over. "Are you all right?" he asks.

The girl finally notices us and bounces

right off the seesaw. She says something to him and Pockets nods. "I promise you won't be stuck here much longer," he assures her. I'm not sure how he can say that with any confidence.

She nods gratefully, and then she and Penny go running off to the slide. (Well, Penny runs. Bubble Girl rolls.) Pockets turns back to us. "She cracked her bubble on her way out of Simon's. Earth's air is slowly causing her some, er, troubling side effects."

"Oh, no!" I cry out. "Is she going to be okay?"

"Apparently the moisture in the air is making her hair frizzy," he says with a noticeable roll of his eyes. "So yes, I think she'll live."

We watch Penny and Bubble Girl as they laugh and slide and Bubble Girl gives Penny a ride on top of her bubble. Pockets checks his watch, then looks behind me and frowns.

We turn around and watch, mouths open, as Feemus climbs back out of his tiny spaceship!

I look from Pockets to Feemus to the spaceship and back again. "But how did he...? When did he...?" Now I sound like Pockets when he was on the phone this morning! I collect myself enough to ask Feemus, "Where's Agent Zell?"

"I delivered him to ISF headquarters, dropped off the cup as instructed, retrofitted my ship so the nav won't be dependent on the satellites anymore, and returned."

Feemus shrugs like it's no big deal that he only left *ten minutes ago*.

Dad is still clearly confused, too. "I don't get it."

"Remember Feemus can play around with time and memory," Pockets says, a little exasperated. "It only *feels* like ten minutes. And now he will escort the girl back to her planet."

I guess he knew Bubble Girl would leave soon after all. I can't help peeking into the ship to make sure that the B.U.R.P. agent is really gone. Yup, he's gone. But in his place are Pockets' suitcase and boxes, piled up in the middle of the ship! I whirl back around, suddenly fearing that Bubble Girl isn't the only one leaving the planet. "Why does Feemus have those?"

Pockets closes his eyes for a long minute. I almost think he's fallen asleep! When he opens them, they're red. I start to get nervous.

"I'm sorry I didn't tell you," he begins, and my pulse quickens even more. "Since the capture of the *Galactic*, crime in the universe has been at an all-time low. Father has called me back to Friskopolus. He feels my time is not well spent here on Earth in between the now-rare missions, and I could be useful in studying the *Galactic* and searching for Sebastian."

So that's why he's been acting so secretive and sad. I want to argue. I want to point out that we DO need him here, that he just captured a B.U.R.P. agent, so clearly crime is not totally gone. The head of B.U.R.P. is probably very good at hiding. It could take Pockets months to find him. Or years! I want to tell Pockets that he is my best friend, and what about Penny? She'll be crushed if he leaves, especially now that she knows he can talk.

But how can I make him feel bad? He has an important job to do. We knew we wouldn't get to keep him here with us forever. So instead of saying anything, I just run up and hug him and don't let go.

As though sensing the mood has changed, Penny stops sliding and runs over. She takes one look at the luggage and me hugging Pockets and bursts into tears. Instead of running to Pockets, though, she runs to Mom, who picks her up and holds her.

"You and your father are still ISF

deputies," Pockets says, patting my back awkwardly with his paws. "We shall meet again."

I reluctantly let go and he turns to Penny. He opens one paw to reveal the plastic four-leaf clover she gave him for luck on our last mission. "I will treasure this forever," he tells her, tucking it into a chest pocket and patting it lovingly. Penny and I cry harder.

Finally Penny gives Bubble Girl a hug good-bye, which looks funny because of the bubble between them, but I'm not feeling much like laughing. Then Bubble Girl rolls into the spaceship, followed by Feemus and then Pockets.

Me and Mom and Penny and Dad watch as the tiny spaceship lifts off the ground and zips back into the sky. In the blink of an eye, Pockets is gone.

The solar storm lasts two more days. With the flying ban lifted, we can finally get back to work, and that means getting Toe back home. Having him around has made Pockets' absence a little easier to bear. Just a little. Penny couldn't sleep without Pockets at the foot of her bed, so I slept there instead.

Dad, Toe, and I climb into the taxi. Penny stands on her tiptoes and leans in through the window. She drops three brown-bag lunches in my lap and says, "Don't forget to eat."

Mom has to stifle a laugh. Penny has taken over her job!

It's my first time back in the taxi since Pockets left, and I keep glancing in the backseat for him. Even though he didn't always come along on Dad's day jobs, I still always felt him nearby. But now even the clumps of fur he left behind everywhere are gone from the seats. All the taxis were cleaned and vacuumed during the grounding, since the space taxi repairmen didn't have anything else to do.

As I root around on the floor for the tube with my space map in it, my hand closes on a tiny disc, not much bigger than a button. I lift it up and look closely at it. The words PRESS HERE are etched across the center. Unsure what to make of it, I press as instructed. At first only static comes through a tiny speaker in

the center of the disc, and I figure whatever it is, it's broken. But then the static
clears up.

"Hello, Archie," a boy's voice says. "I
believe I know why we look so much alike.
Meet me if you dare. Bring the cat."

At any other time, hearing the leader
of B.U.R.P.'s voice in our taxi would make
me jump out of my seat. But I'm too excited
to be scared. I turn to Dad and beam.
"Sebastian wants me to bring the cat!"

Dad grins back. "Looks like the crime-
fighting team of Morningstar, Morningstar, and Pockets the cat will soon be back
together!"

We high-five and strap ourselves in.
"Maybe Penny can come along."

"Not sure how your mom would feel

about that," Dad replies, revving the engine. "Ready for takeoff?"

I open my map. "Always."

We begin our climb into the wide, blue sky. And in the backseat, Toe begins to hum.

THREE SCIENCE FACTS to IMPRESS YOUR FRIENDS and TEACHERS

1. Solar activity. In this adventure, a massive solar flare disables almost all electronic and communication devices. Solar flares are explosions of energy on the sun that launch gases, plasma, and radiation like gamma rays and X-rays into the sun's atmosphere that can reach far into space toward Earth. The one in this story is an extreme example of an X-class flare, the biggest class of solar flare. These solar flares have been known to shut down communications around the world and are followed by intense solar storms.

2. The higher in orbit a **SateLLite** is stationed, the more likely it is to be damaged by a solar flare. A satellite is anything that orbits a planet or star, like our moon is a satellite of Earth. Humans have put hundreds of man-made satellites into Earth's orbit for different reasons. These satellites are used to study the Earth and outer space, provide information on weather, enable navigation systems that help us reach our destinations, and allow us to communicate over vast distances.

3. ELEMENTS IN OUR ATMOSPHERE.

When life on Earth was first developing, tiny creatures in the water and then plants gave off oxygen that filled the air. Humans need oxygen to survive, but on Bubble Girl's planet, inhabitants are allergic to it. When scientists look for planets that may have life, they use instruments that tell us about the atmosphere there. If we find that the atmosphere has oxygen, then there might be plant life. And where there's plant life...maybe there are people! Or as we would refer to them on Earth, *aliens*!

Elise Gravel

WENDY MASS has written lots of books for kids, including the *New York Times* bestselling Candymakers series, *Every Soul a Star*, and *Pi in the Sky*. MICHAEL BRAWER is a teacher who drives space taxis on the side. They live in New Jersey with their two kids, two cats, and one puppy, none of whom have left the solar system.